Shanghai Whispers
Shanghai Screams

Scott Shaw

Buddha Rose Publications

Library of Congress
Cataloging-in-Publication Data
Shaw, Scott
Shanghai Whispers Shanghai Screams
BD836,S546 1990 119-dc78 90-6326

ISBN: 18777792268
ISBN-13: 978-1877792267

Printed in the United States of America

Table of Contents

PART I

I just had enough time after I had pulled myself out of bed, at the break of noon, to head on over and have some coffee or should I say *'cohi'* at this little place *'Victoria'* I like to hit over in the Roppongi section of Tokyo. Yeah, right there at the intersection of the Roppongi crossing.

So me, well, I grabbed the subway not far from my high rise hotel in the Shinjuku sky, Hilton International, and motored my way on over to, *"Cohi dozo."*

It sure went down right. I don't know what it is; some places just seem to brew that bad java.

I sat back, *cohi* in hand, watched as the Tokyo masses passed. Me, I contemplated life, wrote a poem or three, and lost myself into the dream and the wonder of what was to come next in the journeys of and for my life; "Life On the Hard Road," as I like to call it - journeying the Asian extremities and all...

Well, so as it goes, nothing too much to document of the sitting and the watching of the Tokyo mega-life passing by. Some Western homeboy, no doubt via the European sector, had strutted his bad-self in the jute joint and had planted himself at the old *telephono* and he did rap some very bad

Nehongo, (Japanese); way better then me. Kinda pissed me off, but so as it goes.

I hopped a ride back to my hotel in the sky, grabbed my bag, and headed, via the limousine bus, to old Narita International Airport.

Bus Ride, I sat in my usual seat, my one of pre-fer-ence, the first one to the right, right behind the driver, front and center - a better view and all, you know. Next to me, well, not exactly next to me, I rode solo... But, the two seats next to me in the same row, there sat these two locals: one man, Tokyo style, cheap blue suit; and a lady, looked almost like a dyke - buff, you know what I mean. But anyway, I heard them speaking, they were both on their way to L.A. Yeah L.A., my birthplace, home-base, home-town. The place I just did not want to be. I way far preferred it over here in Asia, where any dream is just so fucking haveable. Anyway, they were rap'n in their native tongue about this, that, here, there, travel and the etc. Then they got onto the subject of India; a place, a subject I know too well. I don't know what it was, just their limited observations and their stupid analogies; but the whole subject matter of their discussion kinda pissed me off. I guess that was pissed me off part two in this day.

Like a fool, I allowing myself to be influenced by the comments of others. It is like here, right now as I type - yes, relive this story upon the written page; well actually upon a lap top computer, on board an airplane, forty thousand miles in the sky. Yeah, the dude up in front of me complains about the sound of my typing keys to the cabin steward. I mean give me a fucking break. I got this bad boy soul-ly for the reason of being able to create on the path of the journey. Like what am I suppose to do here, as I journey LAX to BKK, (Bangkok), you know. I don't know this world is a fucking weird place. But, the steward, relatively cool, probably a homo, gave me the way go ahead and told asshole to, "Fuck off." So, fuck that guy. I mean like, the literature must be created and all… And, the demons of the arts are always at the dreamer's throat. Why do we let others control our mind, our space? And for these First Class prices…

Anyway, back to the tale at hand. So, they *rap'd* and I was chill factor zero. But, like with the opinion of the soul boy complaining up in front of me, there is not a God Damned thing you can do about it.

Never-the-less, I made it to the airport in the basic shape of the AOK and slid on through: check in, customs, and onto the First Class Lounge. Nothing much to mention.

It came, the time to board the plane. I always hate it at Narita gate 48, or for that matter at any airport, when their jet way gates are all full and you have to go and take that basic bus ride through Hell to the airplane. You know, where the six zillion people try to crowd through the lines and onto the bus. And, a First Class ticket don't-mean-shit. Well, it isn't so bad if some babe is riding up tight, you know. But, that's another story, another city...

Anyway, I was chilling my way onto the gate and thus onto the perspective bus which would take me to the perspective plane. Next to me, pushing her way forward was this semi-babe of a chick on the white bread side of the picture. Brown hair, shoulder length, skin that had seen one too many days in the sun. A long skirt, birkenstocks, sunglasses, and a dream in her eyes.

Yeah, I could see it right through the sunglasses.

We both made it to the door at the same time, and me being the gentleman that I am, I, of course, let her go through first.

"I was going to kick you if you didn't let me in first."

I wanted to say, "Maybe you would have tried, baby." But, I kept my mouth shut and chilled back.

So, were spoken the words, the beginning of the end if you will. Anyway, my move was in the motion, you know, and, thus, we went into the basic *convo*. The basic nothing discussion that leads to all of this type of literature and all of the *Power Movements* of this world.

Meg was her name. SF (San Francisco) was her city. Yeah, she was in the basic mode of getting the dump by a dude. And, like, you know, how some babes go and get a new *'do'* when they get the dump, others go and become a slut, and her, well, I guess that she had some change saved and put her move onto, towards her ultimate destination, Singapore.

Actually, if you want to know the facts to be exact, as it were, she never actually gave me the word that she was getting the dump. But, like I mean, all the things that she didn't say spelled it out quite clearly. Anyway... It is amazing how much you can learn of a life in just a few passing moments if the right words are put in their place.

So, we exited the bus, boarded onto the aircraft. She was given the direction to the back-jack. She kinda gave me the freak when I was pointed in the direction of the First Class cabin. I mean like hey, yeah sure, you will all get there at the same time but it is all how you get there...

So, placed in my seat, next to me came to plant herself, this mondo-bitch. Mondo, I mean in the terms of her size. Well, let's be real, she wasn't all that fat or all that tall or anything, just hefty enough that it was that, "Look out; stand back-jack." And, that *'do'* that stretch to the puffed, permed, teased realms of reality. She had pulled on with her, this mega big carry on bag. Like bigger than my whole suitcase, man. I mean like, how or why they even let her on with that bad pup is beyond me. To say the least, she did make an entrance.

Basically, she was way nice enough. Her plan, should she decide to accept it, was to make her way to Hong Kong and get her doggies some designer duds made up. I mean like her game plan was to bring this whole line of designer dog clothing back into the States and place it in this shop she was a-opening up on Madison Avenue in the Big Apple. She had the whole thing mapped: had a Bentley, painted red, that was to escort the beaucoup buck dogs to the vets when they were sick, and the etc. She had even brought out a Dog fashion magazine. I mean like fuck me, but come on, they are only animals, and what people do when they have more money than they know what to do with...

So, we spoke, watched the movie, and there the journey/this journey really began.

You know, I believe in signs. No, not just the signs on the road, but to me, my world, well, yours too, all things that are to come are shown, demonstrated to one before they ever come to pass. Is this hard to understand? I don't know? Maybe. I will try to be as brief about this explication as possible. Through my experience, everything that is going to happen to us is pre-shown; we are given a warning, if you will, before it ever takes place. If we are only clear enough to see it. That is the hard part, to understand that something is coming and to be receptive enough to witness the story being told before it takes place.

There is this perfection in this world/in this universe. Of course, we all have choices, but have you ever noticed how, what may happen today, though it may be perceived as negative in its initial impact, later may lead you onto something good, something else, something positive, and important. Yes, I believe in the perfection, though at times our thinking mind; our individual desires may not like to appreciate it. Anyway…

A movie, a space movie, I had seen it before, was on the in flight airline screen. They, the actors, traveled back through time to save their planet; change the process of time, change the outcome.

Remember this movie's subject matter…

That was then. This is now. I am not watching the movie upon an airplane movie screen, I am drinking coffee, in this little out of the way lounge that few guests know about in the Oriental Hotel, Bangkok, Thailand, as I continuing to relive this tale.

The flight was rather uneventful. Landed, and me being who and what I am about; in the baggage claim area, I had to put the look on for the babe, Meg.

I found her over by one of the local telephones trying to figure out how to use it. She was trying to put the call into the local YMCA that she had tried to make a reservation at Stateside. She, as I had been told, previous to boarding the plane in Narita, had done the full on one day: pack everything, stick it in a storage unit, make the reservations for the flight, and bail from SF. In the process, however, she wasn't sure if she had locked up a crib HK (Hong Kong) side.   So, being the gentleman that I am, I told her that if she had any problem with this little barely verging on the *One Star* place which she had reserved that she was more than welcome to come and crib up at my suite.

That is what I dig about this *'one zone de crib'* that I chill at over HK way, they always toss me a suite for the price of a room, just cause I am there all the time.   In all honesty, they are not near as friendly and all way fully happy to see me every time I slice my way on in like the people of the same hotel chain do my way in Tokyo; but then there, they don't toss me free suites either, they just give me my usual room on the top floor of the *e-stab-lish-ment.* Anyway...   I tossed her my card, so she would have no problem getting in touch with me.

"You have a Ph.D.," came the surprised expression from her lips.
"Yeah, that's what it says, Stephen Sexton, Ph.D.   But hey, it's no big deal."

But I could see that to her it was...
Me, not thinking too much further about the subject, I tossed the basic comment, "Hey, even if you do get your

room, if you need someone to hang with, give me the old ring on the tele."

So, the foundation had been set, the move was in play, just kind of a buffer, you know, for HK is one full on party city. I grabbed my bag. I was out-a-there.

I walked out into the fierce pouring, pounding heat of Hong Kong. It takes hold of you; the million degrees of humidity, in a city that never stops; *'ON'* one million hours a day. I went for the line to grab a taxi, placed the ear plugs of my walkman into my ears, cranked up the tunes and me, well I too was *'ON. '*

In the taxi, the driver gave me the basic, "Is this your first time here?" And, all that basic bullshit. "No," was the answer. Leave me the fuck alone was the vibe. But as we drove, there was this tune pounding on the radio, Cantonese tongue. Damn, it blasted. It was good. I even asked the dude who it was.

Yeah, there is this pumping rhythm that goes on in HK, of the local music scene, Canto Pop they call it. It does Rock. Anyway...

We got hung up due to traffic in the tunnel: Kowloon to Central. It took about thirty-five to reach my desired destiny and place of plant-ation. I checked it on in. And damned, if they didn't slice me up a suite again.

I was leading on up to it, mirrored elevator. It's kinda like the feel'n of coming home. More home than I ever knew.

Inside, had the usual guy come to my room, a few minutes later, and bring me a pot of the local tea. And, like always, he gives me the basic rap of the town, of this city, all for the basic tip to be placed in his basic hand. Well, I can play.

I mean like here I was again, in this kill hotel suite. It was almost like a joke for though I have a crib right on the beach back in the suburbs of L.A. I mean like, fuck me, this place was way nicer and fully bigger. Awh, jet setting, not a dime to my name, but a ton of credit cards. Life, it is a laugh sometimes...

I did the basic unpack of my stuff. I was kinda half way waiting to see if the babe showed. I mean like it was no biggy either way. I had my usual places staked. And, as you may know white bread really isn't my *thAng* anyway.

Just as I was about to bail out to the pagan realms of the night and re-introduce myself to all the wonders that lay beyond these walls, there came a little ring on the old telephone.

"Stephen, did you really mean that I could stay in your room? The "Y," that I thought that I had booked a room in, doesn't have room for me and I can't seem to get any other place."

"Yeah, Hong Kong does fill up. Sure come on over."

"I'm already down stairs."

"Well then, come on up."

I naturally did the quick make the pad look as perfect as possible, you know like drill; romantic: this light off, that light on. Light, just oh so subtlety there. I tried to tune in some soft music radio station, but nothing to be quickly found.

A knock came upon my door. I opened it. She popped on into the pad; possessing this rather duffel looking bag of a thing over her shoulder.

"Where should I put this?"

"Throw it anywhere."

So, to get down to the meat of the action and to avoid the boredom that can come with the build up and waiting for... I flicked on the T.V. We spoke and watched some English dialect STUFF, etc. I offered her a drink or three from the trusty hotel room wet bar. At first she went the route of the old Diet Coke. Then, post my pounding a few on the alcoholic side of the beverage picture, she joined in and popped down a few of the old white wines.

"I'm getting really tired Stephen. I haven't slept for at least forty hours. Do you mind if I go to sleep?"
"Not at all."

By this point I was a bit hammered up anyway, and it was late pushing the one in the AM hour - local time of course. And, I too was more than a bit latched up due to the partying which I had accomplished over Tokyo way, at the Lexington Queen the night before.

"Where shall I sleep, here on the couch?"
"No way. Go ahead, you can sleep in the bedroom."
"Where will you sleep?"
"In the bed, of course."
"I am not that kind of girl, Stephen."
"I'm not that kind of guy either, Meg. Believe me, I'm not after anything. And besides, if you can't trust me there's no one you can trust."

Damn, I would hate to count the amount of times I have used that rap.

So anyway, she did the basic pull a few things out of her bag, hit the head, and made her way in-between the sheet; all while I sat there on the couch and duped myself up a little more on the elixir of the gods.

Post and Present; in I go, the bedroom; take my clothing off, toss them on the floor, pull back the cover and into the sack-jack, I get.

"What are you doing?"
"Nothing, don't worry. I just thought that it would nice if we held each other."

I am going to skip all of the basics and all of the bullshit here, give it to you straight, if you know what I mean. A touch leads to a feel, a feel to an embrace, an embrace to a well... I just slid her panties over to one side and let my wild love *thAng* get into motion.

Eventually, she pulled them off, her panties that is; did a round or two on top and all of that basic, you heard it all before bullshit. Nothing to write home about. Eventually, I passed out.

Awoke to a morning in HK. Damn, I love 'em. The sky; gray, cloud ridden, in the about to rain color of mysticism. The dreams they are all waiting to be born.

I planned, head for the shower. Asked Meg, who was on the chill side of coming down with a hang over, if she wanted to join me. She declined. Hang over... Damn, and from just a few glasses of the grape.

Now, actually, I had planned to give her the bone in the shower. You know, like make it romantic and all... But hey, if they don't want to know, then forget 'em. So, I just rolled her on over and with no questions asked, no prisoner taken, I boned down on her right then/right there. It is kind of fun at times, you know? Like *Wang Chung'n* the bad power pup into a dry beaver.

"What are you doing Stephen? I'm really not in the mood."

Too late, the movement was in motion. Got the wild thing happen in just a few, got her to cum in a few more; you know, like the gentleman that I am. And...

Well, she eventually decided to take the shower with me, where we had to have one more wild slap of the pup. Then, post, we went down, had a little breakfast and me, well I grabbed my passport and was off, down the street, a Chinese visa to obtain.

God Damn, Hong Kong pounds; it's like Manhattan times a million. A billion people going a million miles an hour to nowhere. Watch, and each of their movement's is like the motion of a wave, the touch of the wind; somewhere to nowhere, yet it possesses its own perfection.

I went, filled out the paper work, gave them the basic pictures of myself, and then had the anticipated three days to wait. I walked around a bit, scoped down on the scene; to see what condition the condition was in. Then, decided to head on back to the room and give my little white bread of a momentary infatuation a tour of her first visit to HK.

Back up in the room I found a note on the desk, that she, Meg, had gotten a room at the previously described *no vacancy* abode and she was going to latch up over that direction. She would give me the old buzz on the old tele, later. Well, AOK and later-daze to her too. Yeah, now I could go strut the streets, solo. And, you never know what you will find.

Day turned into night, nothing really much to mention. Hadn't heard from the babe and that was cool too, for I had my little HK haunts that I liked to go and hit. I got duded up for the evening; not that I really dress any different between the day and the night; my typical and traditional way baggy, way too big clothing: sport coat, pants, big clunky shoes, and the etc.   I was out.   I was mobile.

Pulled on into this bar I like to hit on the Central side.   Had my usual preference of poison, a greyhound.   Well actually, I had a few.   Up next to me pulls this guy, not dressed so nice, Western, had three derby 'sky pieces,' (hats), three different colors, one placed strategically inside of the other. All worn atop his head.   Well, first they were atop his head, then they found their way on to the bar.

Anyway, I could tell that he was not local talent for he had to check out the menu, and kind of gave the penny pinching look to the prices. Like hey, if you want to play, you have to pay.

Me, well I drink alone; except in the case when the move for the babe is in motion.   But, "Oh fuck," here comes the small talk.   To summarize, he was from Jersey, live Tokyo, TKO as I like to refer to it, was a street juggler, which explains the brims, and had to bail for a day or two to check back in, *Nehon* side, visa and all. Basically, a nice guy.   But, cramping my style.

I naturally pounded a few more while the story was being told.   He sipped his *brau.*

Everything was going along way smooth, when up pulls this guy in this expensive three piece, smelling like booze. He starts to lay down his rap,

"Are you a musician?"

A question not so uncommon to me. I mean like hey, in fact I was just asked that very question a few ago as I was returning from draining my lizard in the forty thousand foot head. This middle aged chick comes up to me and asks,

"Are you in a band?"
"Or something," my traditional answer to the question(s) I always get; either that one or,
"Are you an artist?"

I guess it's my long hair, numerous earrings, and the etc. Yes, I am. But. . . That has zero to do with zero at this point.
Anyway, he claimed to be the counsel general from Italy and he had this brother who was going to a classical guitar recital this evening and he wanted me to come along. He knew I would enjoy it.

"What do I look like a bitch or something? Fuck off!"

So, that was no-go in my department. The juggler; can't remember his name, but he, on-the-other-hand, wanted to go. He kept trying to persuade me,

"Come on, it will be fun."
"No way, man! This dude is a fucking juiced up nut. It just a'int my scene."

Anyway they bailed. The three piece didn't pay his blll upon exit stage left, however, and the bar keep came up my direction thinking I knew the dude trying to collect the funds.

"No way, man, I don't know who the fuck he is. He says he is the counsel general from Italy."

The bad bar keep just gave the nose in the air look, the kind that only the Chinese can do. And said, "Who cares." Anyway, he, the bartender was my bro, knew my face, so that was that.

As for the juggler, never saw him again.
Me, I was laced enough - the hour was late enough, I headed on over to this disco I tend to hit on the Kowloon side.

Yeah, grabbed the old subway that direction. Inside, I slide my way on in, cool and slow, pulled it on up to the bar and I did wet my lips.

It was a weeknight, not a whole lot of action going on. My brain was just separated enough to not really give a fuck. The bartender was pouring them, the greyhounds, hard, and those plus the numerous I had back on the Central side, well, needless to say, I was inebriated.

There was a couple babes, locals, standing up by the dance floor. You know at one of those thin bars on rails that encircles dance floors worldwide. I scoped them upon their initial entrance. Had to give them a few to chill, was my plan; build up a bit more of the liquid courage, if you catch my meaning, and then make my move.

Too slow, maybe? Destiny, I don't know? But the one, yeah she was the more kill of the two, long haired, long skirt, and the etc. Anyway, she went out and danced, solo. Me, pulling it to-get-her enough went for the move on her friend. The music pumped, the lights flashed, and she, well she said,

"I'm too tired to dance. Wait for my friend, she'll dance with you."

In other words, "No."

I don't know, maybe it was the rejection, maybe it was the drink, maybe the I just didn't care, but I turned and walked straight out that night, like a slapped bitch. I grabbed a taxi; easy enough; made it on back to my hotel, Hilton International; hit the late night/all night restaurant of a like the way cool hang out, had me a burger and a cappuccino, to chill back the hang over no doubt a coming sunrise. Then, hopped on up to my room. Turned on the tube, always hated that word tube, in referring to the T.V., wrote some drunken poetry, the kind I can never read in the morning and, well, yes, I passed out.

The next couple days went ahead with little to mention. The basic drink too much, check out the HK chick scene, and the etc. that I am quite duly noted for. No biggy.

Only thing, there was this movie on the hotel T.V. movie screen. Superman was in it. He wasn't Superman in it, but here was that same actor. He traveled through time and fell in love with this chick. I had seen it, on the silver screen, maybe ten years deep. Time travel, I thought that's interesting, again. . .

Got the visa, purchased the ticket, and was duty bound to make my first entrance into/onto the mainland of China.

PART II

I made it over to the train station via taxi. I was en route for Guangzhou and decide that it would be way cooler to ride the rails for a few hours, than to take to the friendly sky.

The lines were the usual waits and pushes and shoves, generally found on the continent. I pulled onto the train, the only *'quai lo'* (white boy) in tow and that, well that just doesn't bother me. Quite in fact, it is the way I prefer it over Asia way.

I have been to HK way too many times to remember and or count. But, I had never really traveled outside of city central. I was quite surprised to see all of this sprawling land - green, agricultural and the like not too far removed from the central district of HK. I mean like, where the buildings rise a million stories in the sky and like they build more floors atop the old ones.

Anyway the few hours on the train went none to bad except for a local homeboy ordering chicken from the passing sale-child, then eating it, and placing the remaining bones in the clear trash bag which hung on the wall next to my window seat; uck. . .

I took a step into the dragon's mouth; across the border through the customs, out to the awaiting taxi into the realms where the gods died hard long ago, China.

I rode through the town with this young semi on the hip side looking driver. Yeah, he didn't even pay me a moment of mind as I walked up to his taxi, like he didn't even care if I was there. Never said a word to me, as we drove. I LIKED IT.

The people pounded through the almost modern city, just a stones throw from the fashion passion of HK but millions of years apart in the actuality of existence. Bicycles rolled down the streets. Buses, only a few cars, and the masses, the millions of masses, they pumped through the streets like some amoebic dysentery in the veins of a virgin traveler. Life, what does it mean.

I got to my hotel. This very modern *thAng* on the crib side of *suchness*. I checked in. It was the afternoon. I threw my stuff into my room and hit the streets. Another Asian city, another Asian place in time. The rich, the poor, the poverty, the knowledge, the nothing. The same thing in every place that holds one onto the dream of lust and the illusion of humanity.

The sky was cloudy that day. I remember it well. It was back at a time when I used to carry major amounts of cameras with me, documenting the world in this/my time period. Yeah, I had three or four of them over my shoulder in this khaki bag. I walked, I walked, I walked. Then, it hit me: the heat, the pulsing sweat of a cloudy day, where you are just not suppose to feel like this. My body turned entirely to sweat, I was soaked through and through. I guess I had been going too far, too long, too full on. My head got light as I reached this road under construction, at the far side of oblivion. I way almost went down for the count.

There was no one around, save for the occasional passing locals, who just gawked at this white boy of a passer-by chill'n himself on their turf. I am sure they had never seen one this deep. No taxi, no cars, no-where to grab a cold one, *nada,* nothing.

You can not imagine how it feels, well maybe you can, but you are out there in the distance, going down, and there is no one to turn to, no one to lend you a helping hand. Alone is a pulsing anxiety, with a heart like a stone, and a hand holding a gun with a finger on the trigger.

Anyway, I just held myself together, as I have had to do more than a few times out on the hard road. I sat back for awhile on a pile of dirt, on a road somewhere half way in construction progress. Somewhere, some way, but no body, mid-week working on all the piles of road construction equipment.   Finally, I got my shit together and moved on.

I probably had trucked twenty miles by the time I pulled it back up front, back up center to my hotel.   Just kind of had to follow my intuition on how to get back, no real roadmap in hand.   Took awhile…

In, I came; headed over for the little exposed java shop I had seen upon checking in. Decided I'd better wet my lips with a bit of the reason to stay alive: poured down a couple cold ones. Then hit for a cola or two as a back up.

While I was planted, up strolls this little in a uniform chick, whom I guess was the hostess but who had not actually sat me down. Rather cute, well so-so. About five foot nothing, short black hair, a cute little smile and, well just and…

She spoke rather good English, made all of this basic small talk; asked me where I was from, if I was a musician, told me she first thought I must be a girl because of my long hair, and had I ever been to China before. You know, like all the *'Why bother'* sort of stuff that life is made up of.

The English name she had taken on was Corinne, pretty enough name, but that my friends, was basically that…

I hit up to my room, caught some *Z's* and awakened to the on coming night.   You see, the reason I had chosen this particular crib was the fact that it was the only *Five Star* place Guangzhou way that had an in-house disco. Now basically, let's clear something up here, I'm not really a disco sort of guy.   But, I do love to dance and now that the music has more of an alternative blend to it in those abodes, well... AOK, in my book. And, Asia way, chicks, it's the only place; you never know what you will find.

So, I caught a shower, caught some dinner, and slid on into where, how shall I say, the music was happening.

Not much to tell you about, in fact. You see in China, there is this policy, at least there was then and there still is now, who knows what's going on as you are reading this.   But, anyway, there are local hang-outs and the rest are like for foreigners only. Only locals that can hit them are those in possession of the big bucks.

So, aside from this kill babe of a DJ who had this long tail down to her butt and kept dancing around behind the record players, which I must admit I did have more than a few fantasies about, it was just a basically no-go situation. I returned to my room solo.

Day next, I go and have a little on the breakfast side of the picture, in the aforementioned java shop, only to once again be met by sweet young Corinne who proceeded to rap down to me the entire time I am a-savoring my java, my cereal, and my etc.

She discusses the fact that this one mega-rock n' super group had cribbed down at said hotel and that she got to meet them and all that. Actually, they were once very very big but you know how it goes with the years and all; one day your here, the next day your gone. Now, they are lost in the realms of *No-wheres-ville Daddy-O.* They were a couple of fags anyway.

I was off to my day, did the just follow my feeling route that I am into. Man, you just don't know how many way far cool places and cool experience you can have when you just follow the old intuition.

I ended up cruising over by this city river; kinda reminded me of Bangkok. I mean it was so cool; just the whole adventure. First, I started out just following it along the pathway that fringed it, and checking out all of the people and houses; stone house for the most part. Stone faced people, for sure. Except for this one bad lad, fiftyish, wanted me to take his photo. I did. Yeah, I did take a million photos, walking down that river. The color(s); gray wall merging to a gray sky, centered by a brown river. Laundry blowing in the wind: red, green, pink, blue. . .

Following it further, the brown of the water, channeled in by a stone waterway. Following it, took me to this market, outdoors, that was set up to its side. The hanging chickens, ducks, waiting to die. Fish, little eels, swimming their last strokes in plastic and metal wash tubs. I don't know, this was communist China, did they care it was their last strokes? Vegetables, yeah they had some vegies out there too.

So, that was the day, a million slides stored somewhere giving testament to my sightings. Anyway, back at the hotel, I go to have a cold one in the coffee shop, Corinne all over me again. Such is life.

I hung in my room, caught my traditional nap, and awaited the evening to come around. Come around it did. I had dinner up in the revolving restaurant; yes, revolving on the top floor of the hotel of course. Same old...

Then came the time to begin to check the sich out and cruise the realms of the night. I was walking through the mezzanine shops of the hotels, when there in my field of vision, comes a perfect picture of the princess of the night. She even wore black. All the best whores wear black. Yeah, she was *cool'n* too, checking out some of the

Chinese art on the wall. Time to make my move.

"Do you like it?"

She looks at me, smiles, and say that she doesn't speak English. Well, my Chinese was none too good at the time. So, I was thinking, "So much for that." But, to my surprise, she asked me if I would like to go and have some coffee. Sure, nothing like a little rush of the caffeine.

So down we go, I was a bit worried of the reaction that Corinne was going to have, as she obviously was way warm for my form, but as luck would have it, she apparently was off for the evening.

So, my little love princess and I communicated the little that we could. I had my handy Chinese dictionary with me. So, a little *convo* was exchanged.

We came to the conclusion that we both wanted to hit the disco that evening, but as it had not opened up yet, post our java, I suggested that we go pay, (if you know hat I mean - pay), a visit to my room. No problem, she easily agreed.

We pile in the elevator, cruise on up. Enter... We sat back on my couch, talked some more. My eyes found their way down to her legs. I could see that under her black nylons were those, oh so sensual, black Asian leg hairs.

Black like the light. Black like the night. Black like her shoulder length hair. Black - like her dress.

Call me weird, but damn, I love that natural unshaven look. I fully got wood.

I don't really know how that first move of love action was made: her, me? But, the movement was in motion and our lips did meet. You know, its like I don't know because there is always that kind of hesitation in thosefirst encounter type of sit-e-a-tions. Like if your jacked up or something then it all moves forward, but when you are straight...

Once I was on, I wanted it all. I placed the hand *'de love* upon her leg. She chilled me back and gave me the "Later" command. Well, later it would be... Though I was ready now/then.

Another kiss or three and we went on down the elevator and onto the dance floor in question. We moved on... Nothing special, she, like the predominance of indigenous Asian just don't have the moves. But, it was good for me to be dancing again. Kinda made up for my last HK *thAng*.

The local, waiter, entrepreneur, who had befriended me in the place on the evening last came up, and gave me the, "Be careful," command. He told me apparently to be caught with a local babe in a non-local room was way no-go and that I could get in trouble. But danger being my middle name and all... Fuck that.

Funny little story about the bad lad if I may deviate for a moment... He had gotten my room number the night before by my signing the tab. He asked if he could come by and show me this very beautiful Chinese painting which he had for sale. I mean like, fuck me, I did not want to be bothered. But, being the nice guy that I am, I gave the old go ahead, twelve noon rendezvous.

I actually tried to bail just before our appointed meeting time, but he snagged me up in the elevator. So, up to my room and he showed me this way cheap and even dirty scroll painting. Needless to state, I was not interested. I mean, like a lot of times, I would have just gone for it and dished the dude out the bread, just to keep him happy. But, I just was not in the space. "No thanks..." He tried very hard to give me the,

"What if I clean the dirty part off?"
"Thanks, but no thanks."

Anyway... So, back to the evening at hand. We danced for a time then did the basic bail. Zero in a zero world. The elevator went up.

Into my room; we did the basic have a drink, do the exchange of slobs and the so on and etc. Then, the move it was on. *In the sack-jack.* Took her clothing off; and Goddamn, it looked as if her body had been run over by a fucking Mack truck. I mean nothing personal here, but she had more then a few layers of flab. You know the kind where it kinda looks like she had been fully fat and then lost it but the layers of skin remained. I mean like go and get a little fuck'n lypo-suction, babe. It was not like she was unaware of this aforementioned fact. Like she kinda pushed her fully flabby and way stretch marked boobs together, to try to place them in some sort of an upright position.

I don't know, man, it was a weird feeling, you know, like there was a part of me that kind of felt sorry for the babe, and then there was the other, the more macho-istic side that was just way not into this kind of meat. I mean like, *'No fat chicks,'* you know. My dick almost went soft. But, only almost.

Anyway, I put the pedal to the metal and burned a little rubber on her. It was a basic two strikes and I was out. It was like, I didn't even care, man.

Question, "How do you make a woman cum?" Answer, "Who cares!"

Done with my deed, we were a-laying around and I skimmed through my diction to find the words for, "How much." I mean like nothing and I do mean nothing, (as opposed to correct English diction: anything), in this world is free.

Once asked the question, she did the basic go into tears and cry a bit. Yeah, sure, I have heard it all before. Play'n the game, I did the basic calm her down routine. Very false, very false, dude. Then she was in the mode of *'swa-jou.'* You know, like Chinese for sleep, man.

But, once is like never enough for me; especially in the two strikes *departmento.* So, fuck the dreaming, give me lived reality any-time. I pounded her again with the *wild pup of love.* Strike one, Strike two, strike three, keep coming on. I was way into the movement of motion on this pass. I was full on. Fucked her for a good forty-five. She was wheezing and screaming. Finally, her beaver dried up, so I had to cum. Nothing left to do with it, you know…

Come morning time. Played it again. But, even though it went on for maybe thirty I was still full-on, no care.

As the time and the motions to get ready came around, we did the shower *thAng* together; planned to bone down on her again, inside, but... Well, that is not the really important part of the story; you see, post getting cleaned up, I bailed the bathroom for a moment, returned and she was brushing her teeth. Normal enough, you say. But, the *hoe* was fucking brushing her teeth in the toilet. I mean God damn didn't she know how to use the fucking sink.

She suggested that we go and have breakfast at this other, over looking the river, hotel. AOK, always ready for a new dance. So, we motored on over, via taxi. But first, prior to breakfast, she didn't tell me, we had to pay a visit to this local and more then expensive boutique in the said hotel in question. I mean like fuck me, man. No one told me that this was coming. I mean like the *hoe* must have had it all planed. No payment in cash, but... A whore's just a whore. Probably thought I wouldn't consider her one, if I only had to buy her clothes. Wrong!

She goes for the trying on of these seriously fucking ugly, on the glitter side of disco, pants suits. There was this part of me that was real seriously ready to make the bail and go for the door when she was in the dressing room. All this, while the owner of the establishment gives her and or me the serious hot vibes in the negatory sense of the word. I mean like if looks could kill... Well, fuck her.

I was going to slice my way on out-a-there but, then came all the thoughts of paranoia, the being in a foreign land and what she could do, what she would say. You know. In Bangkok I would have slapped her and said, "Fuck off." But, the P.R.C? So, anyway, I chilled back and I mean like, how much could something on the mainland side of China cost anyway, I thought? A lot, as it comes to pass. That fucking disco/glitter looking thing cost me fucking seventy dollars; once the translation, calculations had been made in my mind.

A whore is just a whore. And, maybe she got all teary eyed over my question of, "How much," but, a price, too high a price was paid for that pussy, just the same.

Anyway, her new clothing on; I wonder if this is what she did each night, go get fucked, then go and have the homeboy buy her some new threads. Anyway, I'm obsessing here, sorry. So we sat by the river, had a uck little breakfast, and discussed how she was here in Guangzhou on business, she actually lives in Shenzen, near the HK border. Yeah right.

She showed me pictures of her former boyfriend; I don't know what it is, do chicks really believe that a dude wants to see who had been dipping their cooking in there in the terms of the previous? He was supposedly some T.V. star or something down HK way. Like I really cared.

She wanted a picture of me, I guess to add to her *'dick- list'* of photo-realism, stars she had fucked. What could I do? I snagged one of the bad little photo machine pups, you know like in three minute types; the one's I carry, while on the hard road, just in case one government agency or another desire my likeness. I and tossed it her di-rect-ion.

For literary sake here, it was kind of a nice little restaurant in the mode of a coffee shop on the river, as previously mentioned; the big river, not the small type like I had checked on the day the previous. I watched the boats go by, big ones in the muddy dirty water, and tried to explain to her; (oh yeah, I never mentioned her handle, anyway it was Fu Pin, for what ever that is worth), that I, yeah, even I at one point, used to surf the bad waves California way, once upon a time. She didn't get it. Didn't have the word for surfboard in my dictionary. I drew a picture in my handy, carry everywhere, you know for: thoughts, ideas, poetry, notebook. She still isn't getting it. I guess no surfing allowed in the P.R.C.

Anyway, so much for the breakfast, zero in a zero life. She had mentioned that she would be in Guangzhou for the next three days and then would be heading back homeward, post doing her secretarial duties, and would I like to come along with her back to Shenzhen? Well, sure, I can play too.

"Yeah, I would love to come along with you, and we can spend forever together."

The lies I tell...

Needless to say, we took a taxi ride back to my hotel and she went her way, I went mine. The day and my life was Wide-Open.

I did my usual this and that: walk, photo, and the like. Mostly, I waited for the nighttime, my time to come around. Leave the heat for the shedding polar bears.

The night came, I was getting my groove on. Knock, knock, knock, 8:00 in the PM ish comes the thump upon my door. Well, fuck me. Anyway to make a long story short, as this whole thing, even the memory of it is getting old, she, Fu Pin, was in.

I mean like, what's a guy like me suppose to do? Yeah I introduced her to Mr. Dick, one more time.

She had planned that we were to go and hit this local, one the indigenous side of the Chinese picture, discotheque. It was supposedly just across the way at this all/only Chinese hotel. So, we set out, a-hoofing. Had to pass under the main road, via this tunnel; where my main babe had to hock this mega *loogie.* How feminine, mainland girls can be... Other than that, there was just some of the basic venders who sell their wares late into the night place to the sides of this tunnel. And, the occasional cold stare of dissatisfaction dished out by the occasional local who didn't dig a local chick with a *'la-way,'* (Mandarin slang for White boy). Since we are on the mainland I will use the Mandarin word for 'honky,' even though Cantonese does still have a mega prominence in the former Canton, Guangzhou.

En route, she jacked up the heel, on this pair of high heel shoes which she was wearing. Once in the aforementioned Chinese hotel, which was -quite in fact - just across the main thoroughfare from which my hotel was so neatly placed upon, she made a B-line for this in house shoe store and picked up a new pair. The kid here,

like the fool I am, obviously got the bill. A
little too convenient of a time to fuck up
your shoes, babe.

We moved on into the disco, where
she was met by an apparent friend, on the,
no doubt, hooker side of the coin. I mean
there went all the doubts, if, in fact, there
had been any as to her vocation and her base
location, geographically speaking.

It was suck city there; all the dancing
locals, with an occasional white boy, pulled
on in by his whore-hoe. The music straight
from ten years the previous. I made the
suggestion that we bail and hit back on over
to *dance-ateria,* my hotel's direction; which
we of course did.

You know, I was more then sick of
the whole situation, especially the babe, if
one would choose to call her that. We hit
my place; disco, etc. We sat back for a
moment in a booth, as the dance floor was
empty and I do hate to be the only one on
there exposing the moves of my bad self.
Though I did have a fantasy or thirty about
the DJ chick catching my action and
realizing that this white boy did know how
to groove, but. . .

And, sure man, I realize that it was
really   no-go   in   the   communications
department, but when she got up to dance
alone, something that is not at all uncommon

for Asian chicks, with out even pay'n me no mind, well fuck her. I got up, gave the bitch the bail. Headed up to my room. Put the, "Do Not Disturb." sign on the old door and didn't answer it when she came a-knocking fifteen minutes later. I wonder if it took her that long to realize that I made the bail.

So, I was a free wild young buck on the prowl again.

Come morning time, in the old java shop, Corinne hit on me and asked if I would like to go to a disco with her come evening time. I mean, as she put it, she worked at this place, so understood that she was not allowed to hit the local spot. I said the AOK and did my day. Then, while eating in the spinning restaurant for dinner, I asked the direction of the disco I had been directed to. So, I was showed. Pointed it out, out the spinning window. Now, I have to wonder now, as I had to wonder then, why, in the fuck'n P.R.C. did they build a hotel with a spinning restaurant.

Post getting my eat'n on, I cruised by in the direction of said disco. Walking in the passive humid heat of a Chinese pounding night that could mean no more than everything in a fool's world such as mine. Anyway, she the babe, Corinne, looked none too all that appealing as I walked up to the entrance of the structure; 1920's built, no doubt. Pre, the Cultural Revolution. She stood there in the massive entrance-way, slacks and a blouse; God, I always hated those words…

Inside, the disco was this fucking joke. I mean it was all locals, dancing the jitterbug to this shit beat. There was this big movie screen on one wall, playing Hong Kong Kung Fu videos, and like everyone in the whole fucking place was like doing their little lame moves while fucking watching T.V.! I just stood there, or better put danced there, in disbelief.

Fuck… Can you imagine me, this way far cool of a *'style jockey,'* doing my main boog-a-loo, I mean like a-trying to get down and these people are swaying and watching a fucking video screen. This main squeeze, Corinne, she wasn't too much into images on the screen, but she wanted me to the their, (not mine), fucking jitterbug. I mean give me a fucking break here! This is the mid-tail end of the1980s and she wants to do the jitterbug. Which way to '40s?

I don't know it was just kind of an observation, you know, like that, dance was in vogue just about the time the 'Bamboo Curtain' went up, as it were. I guess it stayed; their only youthful contact to the Western world. But now as that curtain, slowly, with a few reversions comes down, what will come next, the fucking twist?

So, anyway, that was that, there was no way in the fucking world that I was going to jitterbug, so I just let the people stare as the only *'la-way'* got down.

No pussy even to look forward to, she couldn't come back to the hotel with me. And, aside from the comment, "You dance really free," so much for that night.

I taxied her on back to her apartment, where she lived with her parents of course. Then, slid it on back in my way, solo.

I stared out from my hotel room window, over the darkening night of a land so full, so far. I realized that there is nothing to do, nothing one can do, only flow with the suchness into the oblivion that this life ultimately leads to; witnessing the nothing.

I was due to bail the next day, had the flight booked and all, but Corinne asked me if I would accompany her on a bike ride to a park in the afternoon. I don't know, it seemed so appealing, bike riding in the People's Republic and all. So, come the morning I was no-show for my flight; just sat it back in, had the basic breakfast, with Corinne hanging all over me, of course, and just slid into the day until the appropriate time came, to move the motion along.

I was to meet her around the side of the hotel; as previously mentioned it was no-go for employees to be fraternizing with the guests. Anyway, I go around the side of the massive complex, one corner, then to two. There I saw thousands, millions of bicycles lined up; even a guard, Guardian Angeling over them. Saw all that, but no Corinne. So did the basic retrace of my steps, maybe I was at the wrong place at the wrong time; I mean like what else is new... But, no... No Corinne. Even checked my watch, Rolex timepiece; had planned to make the way cool few minute late entrance. I did, but she out cooled me.

Finally, back around the corner the third time; there she was. Basic hellos, etc. She unlocked two bikes; had borrowed some homeboys scoot for me.

"You can ride a bike can't you?" She asks.
"Shit, in L.A. I ride at least twenty-five a day, to stay in shape and all, you know."

Well, I actually didn't say "Shit," but I thought it, you know. And, like it sounds better in terms of my gutter literary style and all...

So, we were off. Rode on, with all Chinese eyes, naturally on us: this white

48

boy, long blond hair blowing in the wind, and this *local-yokle* chick.

She wore a dress today, this day/that day; why I wondered, for she had worn pants the night before. For the sake of all logic, it would only seem appropriate to have it the other way around; pants for the bike, a skirt for going out, etc...

The day was bright and we peddled on; this turn, that turn, over a hill here, down one there. We passed the local broadcasting hill, where all the antennas touched the sky, attempting to keep it from falling down. But, it is only an embrace away. And, you can never buy the sky.

As we rode, I noticed a few black hairs that emerged from under her appropriately short-sleeved underarms. "This may get interesting," I thought. But, I won't go into my like and desires again.

We got to the park. She even paid our way to get in, over my mega protest. In the P.R.C. you gotta pay for everything. We walked around this man made green sludge pond, with some man-placed trees flanking it. Then sat down to have some tea. Tea, drink it from a dirty pot, in dirty glasses. "Oh great," I thought.

We spoke of the nothing, the nothing worth mentioning. I mean like, do you ever get the feeling that you just do not like who you are speaking to. I don't know what it was, well, actually, yeah, I do, she was just so damn pushy, so fucking forward about what she had to say. I don't know, anyway…

"Have you ever kissed anyone Stephen?"

What a question. What could I say?

"Why no, Corinne. Have you?"
"No, I am saving my first kiss for the man I marry."
"That's good. That's the way it should be."

God damn, I don't know how many times I've been dished this rap. They all claim to be a virgin, only to later find that the proof being in the pudding, well, they were not. I don't know why they think it matters anyway. Well, to a Chinese dude, I'm sure it does. But, to a *"la way,"* those times of caring are way passed. But, Corinne, yeah her, I almost believed.

The sun, the picnic table we sat upon. The trees around us; the large pond to our side. Corinne, what a fucking movie.

The dude who's ride I had was on, soon to get off of his shift, we rode on. En route,

"Would you like to marry me, Stephen? I like you very much. You are very beautiful and I would like to go to America with you."
"Oh yes, I like you very much too. And you are very beautiful, of course I would love to marry you."

Yeah, right… Fuck…

Anyway, she had two days off coming, two days from today. She had it all planned that she was going to take me on this boat ride up this river to this nice place, she had never taken anyone before; and, we would have a very nice solitary picnic.

Well sure, I had all the visions of popping that possible cherry. And yeah, it would be nice to go and check some place, new and all. But, karma, destiny, or a fool's passion to be on the road; day next, I booked a flight, bailed in the AM. I don't know, just didn't dig her much…

PART III

Got to the airport, did the basic check in and all. Next destination, Shanghai.

On the plane, next to me sitting, was this additional foreigner; forty-ish, balding. American, no doubt. As it turned out, he was a professor of mathematics, on loan from Stanford. We went into the basic discussion of life, reality, God, San Francisco, the P.R.C., Domino's Pizza, and the perceptions thereof.

"How can you say you love pizza, if you eat Domino's," he said.

You ever meet those kind of people that no matter what you say, think, or know, they try to make you feel wrong/feel stupid? This dude was a prime example. No different than the majority of academics. I mean like, I way far, no doubt, had more experience in Asia than he, but his opinions were just so fucking God-sent. Well, anyway…

So, the plane ride was the plane ride. We landed, got off, got our luggage, got in line. I was at the end; everyone else had been either picked up or had grabbed one of the multi passenger mini-van taxis. The professor had the University car meet him, for all of his holiness and all.

I was left alone, standing in the taxi line. All the cars had gone. I was kinda wondering, "What the fuck do I do now?"

Moment's past. I turned, and just walking from the airport terminal, clothed in a white dress, pulling a red suitcase on wheels: long black hair, white Chinese skin, there she walked, no doubt the physical embodiment of the Goddess of beauty. Our eyes met, our destinies were sealed.

Have you ever felt the experience of looking at someone and just realizing all of the perfection was just handed to you. Like your eyes meet and you just know that they, the person, were all that you were ever looking for. Sure, call it love at first sight, whatever. Like the little stars twinkles in the eyes, you know. But, I mean like God damn, when it hits, it does hit hard.

The arrival airport terminal was old. Well maybe not that old, but worn. Yeah, for sure worn. Single level, a chain link fence boxing off the runway.

We were so alone; her and I. I mean like sure, there had to be people working inside or something, but I couldn't see them. There was just the emptied line, a street, a striped metal dividing pole, trees bordering the distance; her, and I.

She walked up behind me with that smile of perfection upon her lips. Yes, you know, that smile of acceptance.

I stood there lost in my own insecurities and blatant lifestyle inabilities for a time, struggling with the macho that knowingly must emerge, then it came,

"Do you speak English?"

She looked at me with those eyes of a known stranger. Like we had met in a lifetime a thousand incarnations in the past; know but not known. She just smiled, said nothing. I assumed that was her answer. I spoke again,

"Where are you going?"

I mean like I had to try.

Then came another car, the final car, my only hopes for reaching someplace that was no place at all.

I studied the approach of the car, though my mental vision was trained on her. In very broken English she asks,

"Where are you staying?"

Well, it was to be at the only International Chain, Five Star hotel,

Shanghai had to offer at the time, Wa Ting Sheraton. My senses had shifted into high gear.

It was a mini van of a car type of *thAng* that pulled up. Our stuff was piled in the back and we were piled in the back seat. I mean like, can you imagine sitting next to a goddess incarnate. Here I was, The Player's Player and I was shocked into oblivion.

The ride progressed through the outskirts of the Shanghai. I pulled out my aforementioned, bad little Chinese form of a dictionary, which I had picked up down HK way. I tried to pull myself together enough to throw the bad rap this chick's direction.

In all those moments of forced insecurity, when you want it all, need to have it, have found what you are looking for; I don't know, why is it, to the tramps, the meaningless wenches in the night, you can slice up a line that would grease every car at the Indy 500, but when perfection is in your midst, well. . . words are hard to come by.

"What is your name?" (I asked in Mandarin of course).
"Mai Su. What is your name," comes from her lips in very plain dialect.

Just a little note, for you, the reader in question; I'm going to write her words in the most proper English possible. But, keep in mind, that any and all conversations were based in a lot of negotiation in terms of attempting to understand what the other meant to say.

It was a ride into Heaven, as opposed as the rides into Hell that I generally seem to take. We made the smallest bits of conversation; she, Mai Su was full on as obviously into me as I was into her.

En route, through the trees into the city, well the almost outskirts of this city, as the afternoon began to draw to a nearing close, we came to the conclusion that she would enjoy having a little bit of the old dinner with me. AOK. The taxi, drove through the masses of locals which lime up daily/nightly in front of the hotel and stare at it; he let us off in front, my bag, and hers was of course gotten to by the bell men of employment and me, well I, I strutted my bad self on in.

You know, there is always this paranoia out on the hard road; like, is my reservation going to be there. Will I have a place to stay. Will my credit card work, whatever. I guess it is just that, like things can happen out here. They have before. So, I pumped a bit of the paranoia into and or through my veins as I left the safety of my ride and proceeded, with the babe in tow, to the check in counter; registration. Like, it would be a mega big slap in the face if I were to get slapped down with no reservation and no available rooms with the dream goddess in the palm of my hand, you know.

Anyway, all those things, all of those times, how many of them are there when we have all of these thoughts that just do not mean anything at all. What a waste of time.

At the desk, I was checked in.

"Yes Dr. Sexton, your room is ready."

I went into a whole explication, for the sake of my new babe's honor and all that,

No, she was not staying with me, she was just going to join me for dinner and could someone please watch her bag until she was ready to leave.

"We don't normally take possession of luggage of non-guests, Dr. Sexton."

Well, fuck me and fuck that, it went back and forth round and round a bit until finally they, this hotel agreed to keep her red suitcase on wheels behind the bell man's desk until she was *Bails-ville Daddy-O*.

Up to my room we proceeded. The hotel large scale, definitely large scale.; a mega chandler here, a roving, circular staircase there. What did it all mean in a land so repressed.

I window faced out into the Industrial side of the city, the spanning pumping plastered of smoke ridden *Third World - Developing Nation* passion. They poured their filth into the sky. The city spanned out before me, brown with the occasional gray structure, which also looked brown from above. A million tiny hovels, a million mouth's to feed. Moving all moving, while the brown smoke smashed hard into the once blue sky.

Me, my mind was more on the beauty in my presence - less on the unconsciousness of man.

I looked through the hotel guest book *thAng,* seeking the best restaurant in and of the hotel in question. Chinese, well, it seemed appropriate. I went straight for the movement in the upward bound elevator with this babe who had accompanied me on this journey to my room, by my side. On the top we were met by this hostess of a lady who informed me that the restaurant was fully booked for the evening but since I was a hotel guest I had the distinguished honor of having them slice me a table in approx. forty-five. Well, time to kill and money to spill, we went back down to my room.

Now, naturally I was full on in the mode that I should way for sure have been seated there and then and was pissed beyond belief; but...

Into the room, we did the basic get to know one another. I shot a picture or thirty of her. And, we the time, as it tends to do, did pass.

Up to the restaurant we ate, that was basically in the mode of zero. But, the cool is and came, from the full on fact of, man, we must have made one hell of an entrance. I mean like this dude, long blond hair full on baggy clothing and her, this goddess of a Chinese demi-goddess.

Have you ever noticed how just sometimes you feel so damn good, proud going places with certain people. It is all like that perfect fashion accessory. Sure, like I mean you can call it ego, for no doubt, dude, that is what it is based in. But, then most of life is based in ego. You know, it is like then there is the opposite, those individual's that, it doesn't matter how hard they try, they just don't make it. I guess it is the hand you are dealt when you are born/born with. Sad/unfair in a way, cause it effects the rest of your living, the rest of your life. . .

Anyway, we had dinner. Did the small talk of basics. I asked her to marry me. For once in my pathetic life, I was serious. She answered, "Yes."

Awh, life…

We left and held it back down into the room for a time. Me, being the macho based idiot I can be at times, did reflect to memories of Fu Pin and had thought the, well-you know…

I didn't put any moves on this creature of perfection, however, just let it all be as it be.

Now/then, it was pushing the ten o'clock hour; though I invited her to stay, she probably didn't understand me. So, it was bail time; grabbed her red, on the wheels suitcase, from the bell man, and to save her the hassle of the attempts at getting a local taxi, that I had come to learn from her, was *No-where's-ville Daddy-O.* So anyway, I got a company car and went for the ride into the night, my first night in Shanghai, escorting her home.

Shanghai at night it is hypnotizing. The buildings: stone, brick, and mortar stretch to the low levels of the sky. It is brown, verging on the black. Old, very old

- like nothing new has gone in a decade, a century or more.

We motored through these Chinese streets, an essence paved in its pity, lost a million years before.

There were not many people out. No, not now. Some bicycles, some cars; few, very few. A streetlight here, a neon, in Chinese characters sign, there. It was all like a rock video, or a horror movie about to happen.

We sat, her and I, close; not too close. As the air conditioning of the hotel taxi saved us from the nighttime humid summer heat, on the outside edge of nowhere. We spoke little, but our individual intentions were known by the other, we were going toward something. Something, as opposed to meaningless nothing. Something that we had both longed for, for a lifetime or more.

We made plans, that though she had to work tomorrow for a time, she would arrive, and we would go out in the early afternoon.

Finally in the dark, we arrived at her passageway to her door of dreams. Yes, it was a passageway into the abyss, into the unknown, for it was not a door at all, more like a stone cover opening which led back into the darkness where a million lost souls must reside and were wandered, attempting to find what their absence was looking for.

I attempted to get out, escort her to her door; she declined, mentioning the fact of being seen with a foreigner in her neighborhood and all...

"So what," I said.

But, the words didn't mean anything to her. She walked off, I remained in cased/inside, as the taxi drove back distant and far to the realms of the living who come out to play.

The main street that took her to the doorway of the abyss, seemed very, how should I say it, industrial. Like things were assuredly being made there. I don't know, just an observation, because everything in actuality was behind large/tall walls. And, lights were dim. We drove on.

Back in the direction of my hotel, I could see it rising in the skyline as we approached; approached, without the driver ever speaking a word to me. Yeah, there they were again, yes, the people. Fuck'n millions of them. I mean like they were lined up like dogs in heat waiting to get laid. They were just there, staring into the nothing of the something. Like what was this all about, man. I mean like, was something going on, was there going to be a demonstration. I didn't get it, didn't know.

Back in, back up to my room, it was pushing the midnight hour. My view the other side, the industrial side. I was not haunted by their glances, only the dreams of what was to come in the day's that followed.

Me, I was alone. Alone like I had been one too many times before. Alone, a place to love. Alone, a place to hate too…

PART IV

I awoke long before the time Mai Su was appointed to arrive, had a little on the breakfast side of the picture, and then made the B-line for the streets; camera bag in hand. Yeah, all those cameras. Yeah, way back then. Before, I had not yet, see it all - lived way too much. Yeah, back before nothing, *no-thing,* not anything, any longer fazed me. And, promises were still possible.

So, out I went, as I tend to do; seeking out the downtrodden of society, placing myself, once again, in the possible hands of death, and wondering what it all had to do with anything.

Yeah, I made it there, the low side of the city, found it with ease. Witnessed, watched, photographed the morning city coming to life, emerging from their stone houses, framed in the form of pure ascetics with a roof of metal here, a strand of wood there. Paved, the streets, most of them were paved. Dirt, trash, clothing hanging out in the air to dry, Yeah, there was that too. A people, millions of people, a million per each single family, single room dwelling. You could see them oozing out onto the pavement where they bleed their tears onto the silenced ears of the controllers. But, I could hear their scream.

The main streets, the thoroughfares, full; people riding bicycles, busses, an occasional car or two. As they pulsed in the summer heat of humidity, staring at me. Trying to figure this *'la-way'* out. Like, just what the fuck was he doing walking their turf.

Back at the *crib de central,* showered up and got ready for my planned meet. In my clothing bag, this bad little designer canvas and leather pup I had purchased for this outer jaunt, I check, I realized that I had sent my only two brought along sport coats out to the hotel dry cleaners. They had both *way* ate it down Guangzhou way and were in need of a cleaning. In fact, while checking my shirt collection, I realized that I had given the bail to all my cool print top pieces, as well; in the early hours of that morning and I was stuck with just the very functional, outback piece, you know like a million pockets, long sleeves that button up to short sleeve ones, and the etc, green shirt. Now, it is not that this was not a bad lad in it own right, but it is like you know there are times when one wants to make an impression; mega fine chick and all. . .

Anyway, what I had is what I had. That and these bad way baggy green pants. In fact, as I sit here now, 1:23 in the PM, The Oriental Hotel, Bangkok, I am wearing a cousin of just that very pair of pants. Yeah, and I still own the shirt, don't wear it much but... Come to think of it, I am sprouting a pair of the same make a model *New Balance 1300* high level running shoes that I was wearing, then too. Too and two, was it only two years ago? No, more like a hundred.

Anyway, I waited. Something which I am not very good at doing. She was a bit late, but you know all the purposed perfection, the promise and the passion. She got there. Knocked on my door. I let her in. God, she was beautiful.

We spoke for a few and then she led me on out to the heat of the Shanghai summer streets. She had a plan, a place to go, and a purpose. So, we grabbed us a hotel taxi and were off.

First she took me to this Chinese shrine. I was not interested. Then, she took me to this Chinese park; less interested. I mean like what do I fucking look like a fucking tourist. A traveler but never a tourist. I like the streets, you know. Not these plastic persuasions of nothing.

I had all of my cameras. I took pictures of her, not of the other zero shit. And oh yeah, she was dressed beyond cool. Way, out dressed me. And if there is one thing that I hate, that is to be out dressed.

Now, let me put this into perspective for you. It is not that she pounded with the fashion passion of say L.A, Tokyo, London, or even Hong Kong. But, I mean come on, this was the People Republic and long flowing skirts, and elegance, were just not the name of the game.

Back to the story at had, the day was the day, zero. Still I became more and more infatuated with her. We had this driver, a hotel *bad lad,* pick up on payment by my plastic passion, of course. He drove/awaited our every command, our every move.

It was almost amusing, for when she had come to retrieve me from my room earlier, I asked about how we were going to get places and she said that she had that all taken care of. "Well," I thought… But, leave it to the Chinese to be the ultimate in the entrepreneur strata.

It was pushing the late side of the early afternoon, time to fill the belly. Her town, I let her suggest. So, we had the driver, drive. This little, well large place on the concrete brick side of the picture: gray and awesome; like Shanghai, in general, rising into the sky.

We paid the driver off. Well, I paid the driver. Fuck me on the monetary side of the picture; again. It equaled big bucks.

Anyway, so he drove off, money in hand. Us, off and onto the pounding passion of the streets. And, for the first time since I had arrived there, like yeah, I felt good, like to be pounding the streets with this kill babe and the eyes of the world, well at least the eyes of Shanghai upon us.

We walked up that bad, aforementioned building. We rode up in this cheese bag of an elevator, second floor. It was this sprawling cubical chamber, wooden tables, wooden chairs upon the concrete floor. Looked like a *Hell-hole* to me. But...

We sat down, we ordered up, some damn good Chinese food, I have to say. The afternoon sunlight founds its way in through the windows and pounded in its Chinese elegance. There was the treetops of a park that could be seen across the road from this ancient structure. But I, I stared at her, my babe. Her back to the sunlight, it outlined her long black hair, like a halo, which encompassed her face.

Though it haunted my mind, I had worried that this structure would at any moment come a-tumbling down upon my head, or that the food would *stiv* me and sink me into the slow death of botulism, food poisoning, I, none-the-less, looked at her; saw Mai Su's perfection. It was like I shifted into a drug-induced realm, another realm, another space; I was in love with her. (The best loves are always the instant loves). And, I realized that I had no better place to be, then with her in Shanghai.

*   *   *

Out on the streets again, not yet dark, we walked for a time to a place where Mai Su knew that a taxi would be available; a local taxi as opposed to a hotel taxi. It felt so damn good, pounding the streets with all of the afternoon people, not a whitey, 'la-way' in sight. Yeah, the eyes, fell upon me, upon us. Life, my ego, and my love…

We caught a ride over by the Peace Hotel, main-lined it back to my crib central. Pulled in through the masses of on-lookers that had begun to form as the evening was coming on.

To the desk,

"Here is your key Dr. Sexton. So nice to see you again."

Yeah, this babe must have be warm for my form, as well,

"Just call me Stephen."

Into the room, staring into the eyes of love, where can it lead us, where if anywhere at all can it go. Damned, if I knew. But, by the point we had returned to this abode in the Shanghai sky, I had come to this very serious and virtually devastation conclusion; here she was, the girl which I had been seeking my entire life.

You know, no one plays the game better then I. Read my books and you'll understand. As I long ago realized, the right question here, the rightly placed move there and you find only one conclusion; power, possession, at least a moment of that perfection, when my jimmy is wrapped tight in a mummy bag. And, more than just that, the truth is the abyss of living every passion to it ultimate logical limit.

God damn, but she had, style, virtue, if you catch my meaning. You know all my moves set themselves in the mode of freeze down. What could I do, I mean like here I had her back in my room, any other babe, any other time, I would have introduced her to Mr. Dick. But, goddamn, how could I do something like that to her, the dream goddess. I was chill factor zero, what could I even think of doing. I did nothing.

The day passed into the evening, the evening to the later night. We sat in my room, watched a little of the cable T.V.;

something which she had no idea of. I mean the locals and all, zero in the basic T.V. *departmento;* unless of course the parents had been saving their *won* for a time and. . .

I suggested that we hit on and into the local in house/in hotel disco. But, she said that she could not go. I mean like me in all memories of Fu Pin and all felt *no problema,* and you know I do tend to have a bit of attitude that this is MY world. So, we danced around with it a bit. I even went down there and checked, but this asshole of a nothing, who I could buy and sell with a wave of my AMEX platinum card, said,

"No. Must have a special government pass for the local girl."

Fuck him. I guess the locals know where they are permitted and where they are not.

So, we sat around the room some more. And that, my friends was that. Hard to believe coming from me, I know.

Now, I knew they had the basic sign up as they often do, you know like place the word in the guest services brochure, "Please have your guests out before ten in the P. M." But like hey, naturally that does not apply to me.

It was getting a bit late, maybe 10:15, 10:20 or so and she was a bit tired. Personally, I was ready to party. But, this being Shanghai, no-go in that department. So, out the door way went, to take her home. Into the taxi, through the masses of people staring into their dream abyss. I think, I realized it then, that here she was this local girl, being handed the dream of all of this city; namely, shacking up at the best hotel in town. But then I realized it, her style deserved it.

A ride back to her crib; Shanghai-central. As the passion of the night screamed to be let free. This city, one could feel it, one had to know it, and destiny deserved it, as the brick structured ruptured in their forced passivity; there could be no love allowed.

We held hands that night, as we drove through the darkened city. To her door, I did not remove myself from the vehicle. Instead I allowed myself to remain planted, not to cause a stir. She went into the passageway of doom.

We, the driver and I drove back through the city, to the other side of town, the other side of the tracks, if you will. Not a word was spoken. Not a sign was made, only the glow of the neon in the occasionally still opened window, the passing lights of the occasional car. The glow from the street lights at night. We, the only thing to illuminate my vision, but my mind was on the love of this lady, the perfect lady. She was there, in her distant abode. I was here, driving through a city with a driver who would not have understood a word had I spoken it to him.

For a moment as that driving night passed, I thought to get out, go and find where the party be. There had to be one a-partying somewhere, someplace in Shanghai. "No, I can't do that." "I can't just do all of that meaningless partying like I have known so well." "No, not now that I have met this babe of dreams."

Through the standing masses we passed, the driver and I. Into my room in the sky, I went again alone.

PART V

The next day came. We had a meet planned for the early afternoon. I had breakfast alone. Then, I had an idea - *flowers*. Now, I mean all babes had to dig flowers - even over here on the mainland. So, I went down, had the main desk babe, who I believe was digging my scene, I had her write up the direction to said flower shop, in the native language and all. Then, out to the ride factory I went. I sliced up a bad boy who was willing to drive me in the direction. And, off we went.

It was a bit of a drive; almost all the way to Mai Su place. But, with the no-go in the pick her up department, all I could do was hit the place and pick up what there was to pick up. The driver, more than happy faced, wheelman; he slid his on way in with me. In my very basic Chinese, I asked him what he thought was good. We picked some flowers out together. Then, we were back riding mobile.

He spoke a few words of English and we tried to converse. As his dialect was *Shanghai Wa*, the local tongue and the fifty or a hundred words I knew were in the Mandarin, well, what we said to one another did take a lot of explaining. But, damn nice guy. Had to like him.

Back at the hotel, still time to kill and money to spill, I hit out to my place - the streets. I walked in the warm, humid afternoon. The sky it was a cloudy gray. "God damn," I thought, "What was I doing." "What was I doing to her, Mai Su?" "What was I doing to myself?" I mean like here I was, this partied-out, tainted homeboy of an all night man. Out here on the hard road, fueled by plastic passion.

And, I mean, there she was, this perfect poetry: clean, pure. What could I offer her but my eyes of blue? Damn, it was all starting to hit me, my inadequacies, at least in terms of the department of relationships. "God, I should just leave, leave her. She would be far better off without me."

But, she was not with out me. Had she been I probably would have told her. But me, I walked on...

I sat in my returned to room hotel room in the sky, in wait, and wait, and wait some more. I was beginning to boil. She was late, very late. I was pissed, very pissed.

And, in all the boiling moments that time, that life should be lived and it cannot be. All those wasted emotions that mean nothing to the nothing; less to the meaningless, like me. All the life, all the dreams, that go on to *never-never-land*. I guess that's what it means, 'the nothing' cast to those moments.

Anyway, finally there came a knocking upon my door. I chilled back for a moment, to let it come again. Just play the game, the one I play/or played oh so well.

Finally, I opened it. And, there she stood, my dream, my life, my woman. And me, I was too pissed off to know what it was. All I saw was my own anger. Which I did go into; the "Why are you so late?" The, "I am too cool for all of this, why are you doing this to me?" "This is my world, not your..." Etc, etc., etc...

Basically, it was just my insecurities, my power tripping. The Street Kid, still in me, who had to fight for all that he ever got out there on the dark side of *tomorrowland.*

She was full of apologies. I was full of angers. She explained, how she had to ride the bus, and how in Shanghai it was so crowed and took so long, etc., etc. I was still pissed. I took my watch, the one I had purchased just for this journey. It had popped loose on my wrist from all my ranting and raving. It was hanging there, loose, on my wrist. I took it, threw it on the floor.

Again, in all my stupidity, breaking what was mine - my watch and her.

76

You know, that was the last time I ever got really angry at anyone. The last time, I ever let a situation, like *zero's-ville,* control who and or what I was. The last time…

Anyway, eventually, seeing through my own folly; I chilled. And, though it all probably added up to *nada.* It leads me to and or once again past the point of the old. So, I guess that it is worth a line/a word or two here.

I don't really remember how it ended, the anger that is, only that it did. I handed her the flowers. She never had gotten flowers before. She cried.

We spent the day, on the town, in search of this floral Chinese wall hanging I desired. She knew the places. I had the cash. I got it, still have it. It hangs on the wall of my crib back stateside. It now, I suppose is listening to the sound of the waves crashing on the shore outside of my patio window.

I again, that day, strutted my bad stuff with the skill of a kill babe in tow. I laugh, at my own ego…

The day turned to that night, as the day always seem to do. We sat in my room. We drank, together, for the first time, Chinese *'pejoe,'* "Beer." Gotten, from my, in hotel room, refrigerator. We drank it. Her face turned red as so many Asian girls do, allergic reaction to the alcohol. We drank, our lips left the embrace of the glass long enough, and found their way to one another's. Our first kiss. We kissed a long time.

A long time... A long time past, 10:00 of the P of M. She, my dream, looked at her watch. She had to bail.

Though, I was none to disposed to this idea, none-the-less, I got the hotel ride and off we went into the night. She held her flowers close to her. She held my hand.

Now, I'm certainly not claiming anything special. No gifted powers that any one else who grew up on the wrong side of the tracks, as it were, such as I, would not possess. Nothing different - nothing more. But, as the caress of the Shanghai night grew around us; us: Mai Su, the cabby, the taxi, and I; there was this feeling, this other presence, the notice of a following something. Something lost, deep and dark, lighted only by the reflections of the night; as its metal passed under the glow of the occasional neon in a distant and dark window.

We drove through the streets of Shanghai.

Now, my friends, it begins to get weird. For those of you not disposed to the other side of the coin, the mystical side of the picture of life; well, you can pick up your bill at the desk.

As we past, this one gated structure over to the right; the right of the night. It was almost gothic in its form and design. Had this large arch like *thAng,* which guided the entrance into its depths. The gates underneath it were closed.

This stretch of the Shanghai thoroughfare is dark. This structure well lighted; pouncing its vision throughly into the night. Above the arch, is this dragon, carved/etched into the concrete. I looked at it and it was as if, time stood still for a moment; like the taxi was not moving at all. As if Mai Su was not holding onto my hand. It was as if, we were eye to eye; the dragon and me, deadlocked in time.

Then I glanced down, below the gaze of the dragon; the number below it, address, 666. Fuck!

Now, if I can paraphrase here, and interrupt the overall storyline, as I often tend to do. Its like, you know, really a number has nothing to do with *nada,* it is all the definition that one gives it any power. Like, how many times has a number like 428 come up. It comes and goes with out even a notice. But, then there is this number; the digits prescribed as the number of the beast. And, you take notice. Well, at least I do.

So, anyway, time begins to move forward again; we passed it. And, somehow, some way, some destiny was locked into place. There was no way to beat it. At least not yet.

I looked over my shoulder and there it was again; yes, I was right. There was a car following us. A car driving into the night, with its lights off.

We arrived at Mai Su's location. We made the typical U-turn, as continually directed at the driver by Mai Su, to pull up front and central to her crib entrance which would lead her back into the depths of the night. I looked over my shoulder; the other car, like a tractor beam on the Star Ship Enterprise, was in tow.

Sometime, in moments like these, time lasts forever and ever. Other times, time goes by in a flash. She squeezed my hand, bailed the car. The taxi driver drove off in a flash. I looked out of the back window, as the other car pulled up. As the darkness of the night encroached, as we veered around an oncoming turn, I could not see what happened to her.

I asked the driver what was going on. He didn't speak English. I told him to stop;

first in English, then in Chinese; he did not. I screamed, "Stop!" He still drove forward.

By blood pressure soared. My mind raced as he sped, much faster then normal, faster than any driver had done before, down the darkened road. There was no place/no way for me to jump out and go back to

We pasted the dragon again. Our eyes met for the second time.

Now, as I write these words, he tries to capture my mind again. I will not allow it.

Back at the hotel, I go to the desk and ask the night time desk chick, who's warm for my form, "What's up, with all this." She didn't know.

So, I went back up to my room, not knowing what to do with all this intense energy. I had a drink or three and lay there in bed; waiting for the daytime to roll around. Waiting, with the hopes of her, my love Mai Su, coming back, and telling me it was all all right.

PART VI

The day rang through as it tends to do. I sat there, waiting, intense melodrama pounding in my heart; every scenario seen on every 1970's T.V. drama.

This day - late again. The knock came on the door. No games today. I quickly went for it and opened it.

"What happened, last night?"
"What do you mean?"
"With that car, you know?"
"Let's sit down."

As the tears came to her eyes. All the thought of all the pain that man, society, the world, lays down upon a woman raced through my mind.

To skip the small talk, and to get to the point, she told me of how they were the Chinese Secret Police. Something, being the Asian Scholar that I am, I know does exist in a very big, bad way. They had taken her to their main office, and had accused her of being a whore, due to the fact that she was with a Westerner.

"Did they touch you, did that harm you?"
"They broke the flowers you gave me."

Fucking dick-headed assholes. I mean like, why is it, that every culture, every race has to think that they are the best; that they are better then the rest. That there breed is the purest. The most superior. I mean like, in another fucking thousand years, there is only going to be one race, anyway – it will be caramel flavored golden.

As it turns out they didn't 'do' her or anything. Just fucked with her until approx. 4 in the A.M. All due to her hanging with me, past the 10:00 PM bedtime. Fuck!

I was mega pissed. I called up the hotel manager, who came up to my room and gave me the, "I'm sorry, but…." in all of his fifty year old proper British accent. It meant nothing!

Then, we: Mai Su and I, went down to the hotel java shop to dish up a little brunch to hopefully chill down my situation. And, God damn, if the main guy who gave her the main source of bullshit wasn't sitting in there having java with this Chinese young buck dude of a Hotel assistant manager. I plowed right up, in their faces. Demanded an apology. The asshole glorified desk clerk, all thinking he was firm and powerful in his position told me that this was China, and I could complain to whoever I wanted but this secret police guy would not lay me no apology, no way.

"She's going to be my wife, man! I'm going to marry, her!"

You know, this was like one of those situations where you wish you were, or at least the son of, somebody so fucking powerful that you could just show assholes like this where the true power lived. Or, like at least back in the States, pull out your *wammy,* and flat-blast both of those *mutha fuckers.* But, he was right, this was China and there wasn't a goddamned fucking thing that I could do.

Mai Su, obviously very nervous to be there in the java stop, so we bailed. Hit out on the streets, in hopes of finding a brief relief, glimpse of shelter and safety for her. Me, I hoped I would bump into the asshole assistant manager on some lonely desolate Shanghai paved street, where I would take the bitch down. No such luck, not yet anyway…

We walked, her and I, as the day became cloudy; walked to nowhere, (nowhere). I don't know, I was just boiling in my pissed off ness. But there wasn't a thing I could do. I hated being out of control.

As we walked through the stone slab building streets; gray, lined in gray. All built, probably by the Chinese for the

Japanese or the British, way back when. When, Shanghai, this place lost in the bounds of time was an international corrupt port; tittering on the edge of the world.

We held hands, I appeared to be happy and cool. But was not.

We walked through this culturally desolate world; hand in hand; gray everywhere. I reached over and kissed her on the cheek.

Just then, these dudes in a doorway; lean out and begin to talk tough, act tough; called her a whore. A word, in *Shanghai Wa,* I did understand.

"Fuck You!" I said.

I think that the three of them caught my vibe, as I stood straight and tall, ready to kick some serious ass. Mai Su tried to pull me away, but this was just what the doctor ordered to vent my frustration.

I could tell they were a bit shaken, not expecting this *'la way'* to stand up to them. But, hey *mutha fucker,* you wanta talk the talk, let's see if you can walk the walk.

"Step up, *mutha fucker!"*

I broke my handhold from Mai Su and walked in towards the biggest of the three who had now exited the safety of the doorway. I shoved him back.

Its like the typical dude *thAng,* had he been alone he probably wouldn't have done/said anything. He may and thought it... But, with the sidekick dudes, cheering him on. He had to play hard. Well, they don't come any harder than me.

It was pay to play time for him. He didn't know what to do. I could see it in his eyes. But, answered any questions of doubt for him. I shoved him again.

"Put your money where your mouth is, loser!"

The three friends stepped back, in an almost simultaneous fashion. Once a few words were exchanged between them, they came at me.

The first one, the biggest one, swung at me. I stepped back out of the way of the oncoming punch. Then, I full fisted him in the jaw. He went back. He went down. The next oncoming punk attempted to grab at me. But, I got there first - shoved him back and did a stepping side kick to his face. I saw the blood from his mouth and nose splat. He was out and down. The third one, stepped up. I back fisted him three times in the face. He went back. I hook kicked the side of his head, and he too was down and out. The first guy I tagged was getting up. I pointed at him to stay back. He clumsily staggers to his feet and begins to go back into the structure.

To avoid the oncoming family and friends, which who the fuck knows how many of them there would be, I took Mai Su by the hand and we quickly walked into the further gray Shanghai.

My hands, my body, shaking from all the adrenaline that was pumping through my body. Mai Su, asked if I was alright. I was.

"This always happens," I said.

Back at the hotel, back in my room, we sit in between the two double beds that adorned my space. She leans on one, I on the other. We stare aimlessly into each other's eyes.

9:45 rolls around, she is rather insistent that she leave. I guess I understood.

We took a hotel taxi down by the river. In order to fool any maybe following secret cops we get out and walk the streets, walk the flanks of the river, while thousands of locals stare at us. She wore a yellow dress, which I didn't really like. We walked hand in hand.   The night air was warm, verging on hot. Our hands, sweated.

I walked there, proud, strong, glad to be who I was, what I was, for once in my life.   Engulfed in the love of a woman which I dreamed my entire life of finding.

We took a local taxi back to her realm, passing the eyes of the demon. I checked, no following cars.   Reasonably assured that she was AOK, I bailed back and to my room. Sat there in love, lust, dreaming of what was to come.

*   *   *

The next morning I was rudely awakened by this homeboy of some forty year old Chinese dude who had this other dude maid in tow who could speak'a the English. I know because he had cleaned my room before.   Yeah, whatever.   So, fuck me.

This dude, the older one, he went through this rap, that Mai Su had been promised to him and that she was a good girl and should not be seen cavalavanting around with some white boy like me. Yeah, yeah, whatever.

He first tried to break hard with me, play it tough; but don't get tough with me, mutha fucker.   When the loser realized that, he chilled back and tried to play the nice guy. Another attitude which I did not particularly dig.

Anyway, he said his piece. I guess he thought he got what he bargained for. He smiled, shook my hand, like a fish, and bailed.

"God damn," I was thinking, "This whole picture is getting way to muddy for me." I called up, made some reservations for Beijing.

*   *   *

Mai Su showed up at her usual late appointed time. I explained to her the *sich.* She went way into this whole thing; first, "No, no, no. I don't know man" Then the, "This is my life. I can marry who I want" What do you do?

We sat in my room all that day. I guess afraid to go out and face what may happen next. We sat there, between my two beds. I fell in love with her, all over again.

And, the dude, I am, and I guess I will always be, told me to, *'Wham- bam thank you mame,'* nail her. As we kissed, I knew that I could have. But, I did not. The fool in me, I guess; save it for another day. When we are married; forever, forever, forever.

It came time to take her home. I did.
Checked for the posse. Not there, AOK.
Passed the dragon, who seemed to be
laughing at me. I looked back.

Morning, next, Mai Su, shows up at
the crib, unexpectedly, way early.   Wanted
to take me to the airport; see me off.
Though I didn't think this was too cool -
whatever...

Taxi ride there, zero. Airport, I go up
and as all the locals wait in line; I by pass
them and go straight for the gate.   Mai Su,
afraid to kiss me in public. I let her go with
just a warm grip of my hand. I fly to Beijing,
not knowing what to do; what will come
next.

PART VII

Beijing was kicking. I had this disco latched up right in my hotel. And the first night in there was pounding. All of these exchange students via Beijing University.

I latched onto a semi babe of this chick form Switzerland. She was twenty-seven; so knew what she had and knew how to use it. We danced and dance. The first and only time in my; thus far life, where I sweated so much, that it was like, it just turned off. Like, no more sweat man. But, I kept dancing - had to - though I knew that this situation had to be none too cool.

Anyway, the chick cribbed. I won't go into unncessary details. But, not bad for a white chick. The morning came, never saw or heard from her again, oh well.

My mind stayed on Mai Su. I guess, how could it not. I danced around Beijing, to the zero. I even called my mother and told her of this new found love, how she was so perfect.

Her, my own mother, in all of her negativity; it was like a knife that I felt stabbing into my soul,

"She's not a good girl. There's a lot of ways a girl can fake it."

"But, no, not her. She's different."

But, it was like it all happened there/then. Like somehow, some way, she, my mother, set the negative vibes in motion; assured the dragon's course of destruction; she, her word's took away any chance I had of being Okay, normal, of being in love, being for real.

It's like, I felt it go. I could feel it being stolen. It was like a physical sensation as I was on the telephone. I hung up. I had to go back to Shanghai.

*   *   *

I caught a plane the next day; and though I left the party central of Beijing, it was love, I sought; forever love; the kind that is promised in all the movies, on all the T.V. shows.

Back at my hotel, Shanghai, this time with a view of the city, of all the people staring up, in awh. I threw down my suitcase; out the door, got a hotel car. Drive me to the heart of desired destiny. I lead him; turn here, turn there, turn right, left; there to the dark gray abyss, that lead into the realms of where; she Mai Su, lived.

We passed the dragon, he did not look so fierce in the light of day.

We arrived at the gray gateway to the abode of my love. It was like, where to go now? I walked in, and it was like walking through the destinies of time, history, life, love, or the closest thing there of - long mazes of gray concrete dwellings. Lost, living somewhere to no-where

I walked, as all the people stared at me. They looked at this *'la way,'* dressed in a gray Italian sport coat, walking nowhere through the mazes, not really knowing where or how to get there. I doubt that anyone like me had ever paced those streets.

Finally, this old lady looked at me, smiled, took me by the arm - lead me... She pointed at a door; which was at the top of these gray walled encased steps. She let go and smiled. I smiled back. I walked up them.

I stood at the doorway which was at the top; there for more than a moment, thinking, the, "Should I, " "Should I not." I did, I knocked.

Opening the door was this old chubby Chinese lady. She looked me up and down. Then motioned for me to enter.

Inside, it was like a two room crib. No bathroom to be noticed. The main room that I had entered, was dirty off white, maybe 10 X 10. A refrigerator up against the wall.   That meant that they were, "Privileged," I assumed.

There was a bed in the room.   A chubby old Chinese dude sitting on a chair. He looked to be placed somewhere, lost and alone, straight out of the 1940s.   He looked me up and down from that chair.

The old lady pointed to the other room.   No door between them, just space, air. I walked in.   And, there she lay upon a single bed; Mai Su, alone.

Something was wrong.   Her face was stained from the sign of too many cried tears.   Asleep, she woke to my presence. She opened her eyes, looked at me, and begun to cry again.   Quickly, I went to the bed, and sat on in.

"What's the matter?"

As the tears proceeded, as the time continued, as her mother looked on at me in disgust from the door jam, Mai Su, explained to me, how, now, I would never want her, never take her away from this place.   For now, a man, that promised man, who had come to my hotel, several days the previous, had followed her in the darkness. Followed her to the depths of the abyss. And then, when she was alone, he took her. He had her.   He took her, so no other man would never want her – she would be soiled for life.

I don't think that words can ever explain that feeling. That emotion of a woman you love being forceable taken from you. That pain, that saddens, that frustration, that rage, that sorrow that you were not there to save her. Even for me, the hard-boiled son of a bitch that I am, I too was lost in the pain.

I don't know, in all of her tears, I think I cried too.

Her mother walked up to me, handed me a cup of tea. "Thanks but no thanks."

*   *   *

I flashed back to a moment, many years the previous. A moment lost in time, lost to the realms of 1970s Hollywood – Hollywood, California. I had a girlfriend. We were in high school together. There was an old-lady rapist on the loose in Hollywood. One Saturday morning I went to pick her up – my girlfriend. The night before her grandmother had been hit by that fucking loser. She, my girlfriend, wanted to go see her. She did not yet have a car. I drove her - lost in the realms of trepidation - not wanting to go - not being sure of what I would find. I had never met her before.

We went. We met. She, the grandmother, invited us to an Old Chinese restaurant on Virgil Avenue. We ate. She needed a moment not to be - to forget.

We finished. I tried to pay. She would not let me. She paid. I drove her home. My life went on. I knew her life would never be the same. The old-lady rapist was eventually caught. But, how many lives did he destroy based in a soulless act, formed from nothing more than desire?

*   *   *

Shanghai, it was like I fully didn't know what to do. I wanted to kill the guy, but I didn't even know where he was. He was obviously too much of a pussy to face me. He was hiding out there in the netherworld, hiding among the masses, afraid to show his face.

Violence was all I knew. It was the only cure. Had I found him, if I ever find him, there will be violence.

I looked around me and watched the face of her parents. I saw how they were kinda pissed - kinda, but not really. For he was the dude, the dude that they had laid her life down on paper as owner, propriter. How many years ago was that? How unfair can that be? For them, her parents, he had just dipped his dipstick, attempting guide fate. To take control over a person, an emotion, a life, he had no right to dominate. He was trying to steal her away from me.

"I screamed but nobody helped me," she said. "I wanted it to be you."

As the tears flowed down her face.

"Now you will never want me. Stephen, I love you so much."

Man, there is nothing lower then a dude who rapes a chick. I always promised never to write about it - never to propagate the words. But, here it had happened. And, I realized that there wasn't a goddamned thing I could do about it.

She lay in bed. It had all been taken from her. I tried to convince her that it did not matter. But in my heart, I was just as destroyed as her.

Eventually, I left her room. Left her to cry herself back to sleep.

I found my way back to the hotel car. I passed the dragon as we drove through the Shanghai streets. He appeared to laugh. I went back to my hotel room, called my mother; woke her from her sleep, screamed at her, at how her negative vibes had destroyed the perfect love. The perfect love that I almost had the chance to live. Again, I hung up.

I lay in bed that night, trying attempting to somehow change reality, to make it all different. I tried but there was nothing I could do.

My mother called me back late that night; probably sometimes in the realms of her day. She told me that it would be alright. It would all work out. I could marry her, and somehow forget. I hung up on her again.

*   *   *

The next day, as I lay there still in my bed; came a knock upon my hotel room door. I reluctantly got up to answer it. There she stood Mai Su, appearing like a beaten puppy dog - lost and all alone.

When I let her in, she grabbed on to me - like she could not believe that I still wanted to know her. She held me so tight. That hold went on for several more weeks as time past to the abyss that life has now has all come to be.

I didn't want her to have to go back to that place, that realm of gray stone building that mazed itself into nowhere and nothing -

past the venom of the dragon - out there where the Secret Police follow your car with their lights off. Assholes, afraid to show their face. I wanted her to be safe, protected within my arms.

We rarely went out in those days. We stayed in, watched T.V., drank the *'pejoe,'* (the Chinese beer) stocked in the hotel refrigerator. Held each other, occasionally kissed. I wanted her to know that her body was not what I was after, that I loved her, even though.

*   *   *

I had a friend send me my birth certificate. Had her send me a paper from the State of California, stating that I was not married. All this at the prescription of the government of the People's Republic of China. All this to marry one of their twenty billion people. It seemed so foolish, as we would go to the American Embassy and she would have to wait outside while I would attempt to get/try to get the permission to marry her so we could leave this lost land; forever. There was always some new bullshit, new stipulation or regulation they would come up with...

One day, one of those visited the embassy days; I left her out in front of the gray stonewalls which surrounded the place. I suppose they were constructed so the insiders would feel secure - would not be threatened by the massive outsides - those of a different blood.

I went inside. I had to leave her outside. She stood in the crowd of the Chinese masses that waited there each day. And, though her beauty made her stood out. I left her there. I went in.

As I walked through the gates, the gate that only an American can pass through, I thought about forever. I thought about us, together forever. Forever, only a fool uses such a word.

I exited the embassy, no further along then when I had gone in. China, twenty billion and they do not want to allow even one to leave.

I looked she was not there. I looked all around. No bathrooms to go to, no place to hide from the sun. What had happened! I was frantic. Nobody knew.

I raced back to the hotel. She was not there. Frantic, I pounded through the streets of Shanghai in the direction of her parent's crib. I mean, have you ever lived those moment when every second seems like an eternity - heart pounding, thoughts racing to nowhere? This was one of those moments.

I didn't want to look at the dragon. But, as I passed, the dragon looked at me.

At her place, no one was there. I stumbled back through the maze, to the street, to my cab.

Back at the hotel, I called up the Brit hotel manager asked him if he knew what was going down.

"Maybe she went back with her own people."

"Fuck you," I said.

The day turned to the night as I waited for her to return. I scanned the psychic airwaves trying, attempting to call her back to me. Attempting to find out where she was. The night turned into the day and though I used every psychic contact technique I had, all that came was the vision of the dragon and an old Chinese man - ancient.

For those of you who may not know me - know my, for what ever destine reason, path of life. It falls to the realms of the cruising the realms of spiritualism - understanding and transverse the ultimate reason for WHY.

With nowhere left to go, I returned to her parent's abode a second time. The door was answered, met by none too happy faces;

tears that rang through the sounds of the mazes of silence. The gray stone walls which plastered against the dream.

A Chinese man - her older brother as it turned out, told me that they, the Secret Police, had taken her from outside the American Embassy. And, when she would not give them her body freely - the body they considered to be the flesh of a white man's, whore - in their attempts to have it, they took her life. Took her essence away. Took all that ever was – ever could be.

As I yelled scream and generally freaked out, he told me it was the P.R.C. There was nothing anyone could do.

PART VIII

Dead, she had been killed. And, in China, no way was a government official going to answer for dick.

They all blamed me: her brother, her family. They were probably right. Had I never known her, never attempted to walk down the path of *'promise me forever love'* then she would have never dreamt, never been cast to the world of sin. Never known, thus she would have never suffered.

*   *   *

I left Shanghai, where I obviously was not wanted - not meant to be. I caught a plane back to Hong Kong.

I remember those nights as I sat there in my HK hotel room. Those nights, knowing the only way to change anything was to transverse the bounds of time.

I had heard of some techniques. Studied them long ago. But, actually paid them little mind. Even watched them in a movie – no, two movies - one on an airplane, one in an Egyptian hotel room.

I used everything that I had - placing myself in the time, space, reference of all that could move, must be able to move, to pass through these limited realms of human perception.

Yes, I knew, as Siddhartha Guatama, the Sakyamuni Buddha had said, *"The cause of suffering is desire."* I had watched it first hand - witnessed it all the way through. This desire was destroying me - just as desire had destroyed her, Mai Su.

Into the ethereal realms I moved. I could see the time, as it was before her death. I knew if I could get back, penetrate that time zone, before it happened, then I could save her life. I knew I could do it! It would be as if it never was - never had occurred. Only I would know, what had gone down. Only I would be left holding the truth. But, I knew I could be that strong - keep that secret. Hold the change of time, the revamping of existence. Yes, I could do that. And, the rest of the world would never know. Even Mai Su, she would not know. She would be changed. She would be saved. It would be changed. And, all would be as it should have been.

Each night, in the dark, with the sounds of Hong Kong rumbling outside my window, I would move into the space. I could see/feel the time. It my mind, it was transversable. All that held me back were those evil demons - a laughing dragon and an ancient Chinese man.

I called to all of my psychic allies for help. These old men, ancient ethereal beings, from a group I belong to - sourced back in the States. On this spiritual plane, they sat behind an alter. They were the strongest of guides, the closest of ethereal allies. They were there in the cosmic realm with me. But, even they did not have the strength to break through. They whispered to me across the secret realms of non-physical existence. They told me they could not help. They spoke that the dark embedded curse that lingers from ages of sorcery across China could not be overcome. Not here. Not this close to the source. The curse, it kept me from transverse time. I could not fix the broken.

*   *   *

That was it. I couldn't do it. I knew that if I had continued to try, I would have gone insane. So, I let the desire go. Leaving her, Mai Su, to rest in hopefully a better place.

Since I left that place, that space, I have never believed that anything in life matters. Not since then. Not since that place. A long time ago...

And, if I ever find the techniques, I will lay them down for the adepts. List them in *'Secrets of the Sect.'* But, for now/for then, the physical destiny remains all that manipulates time.

Scott Shaw
2 April 1990
The Oriental Hotel
Bangkok, Thailand

About the Author:

Scott Shaw, Ph.D. is a native of Los Angeles, California. He is an artist, author, poet, musician, photographer, filmmaker, mystic, and scholar. He makes his home at the Pacific Ocean creating art and travels the world living enlightenment.